小一郎ぎつね
Fox Koichiro

作者	森本マリア	Written by Maria Morimoto
翻訳 翻訳チェック	小泉直子 ジム・ロナルド ナンシー・ロス	Translated into English By Naoko Koizumi With assistance from Jim Ronald and Nancy H. Ross
立体挿絵	彩瀬ひよ子	Figures by Hiyoko Ayase

小一郎ぎつね　　もくじ
Koichiro Fox　　Contents

ゆきちゃん　4
Yuki　5

稲荷のキツネ　6
Fox in the *Inari* Shrine　7

オシッコがしたくなる　8
The Urge to Pee　9

オレンジ色の火　10
Orange Flames　11

ねとぼける　12
Half-asleep　13

不思議な話　14
A Mysterious Story　15

逆立った髪の毛　16
Hair Standing on End　17

うわさ　18
Rumors　19

小一郎　20
Koichiro　21

ふえたキツネ　22
More Foxes　23

いも団子　24
Potato Dumplings　24

ヨトウ虫　　26
Cutworms　27

いたずら　　30
Tricks　31

消えたキツネ火　　32
No More Fox Fires　33

化けの皮　　34
Truth Revealed　35

ほんのり、しあわせ　　36
Small Happiness　36

ピカドン　　40
Pikadon　40

丸子山の稲荷神社　　44
Inari Shrine on Marukoyama Hill　45

永遠の鳴き声　　46
Eternal Voice　47

あとがき　　48
Afterword　49

カバーデザイン　稲岡健吾

ゆきちゃん

　ゆきちゃんが子どもだったころは、第二次世界大戦のさなかでした。

　食べるものも着るものも履く靴もなくて、みんな貧しい暮らしをしていました。

　懐中電灯の電池もちょうちん用のロウソクもないので、月の出ない夜は暗て外が歩けません。

　村役場のサイレンは警戒警報や空襲警報を鳴らして、敵の大型爆撃機B29が近くまで来ていると知らせていました。

　晴れた夜も曇った夜も、空を何本ものサーチライトがぐるぐる回って敵の飛行機を監視していました。

　灯火管制がしかれて、どこの家でも電灯の傘に黒い布をかぶせ、一筋の明かりも外に漏らさないようにして暮らしていました。

　でも、澄んだ空は星がきらきら光っていて、とてもきれいでした。

Yuki

During Yuki's childhood, the Second World War was going on.

Everyone was having a hard time – not enough food or clothes and no shoes to wear.

There were no batteries for flashlights or candles for lanterns either, so it was too dark to walk outside on nights when there was no moon.

The sirens of the village hall went off from time to time for air-raid warnings and yellow alerts to warn the villagers that the enemy's large B-29 bombers were approaching.

Every night, whether it was clear or cloudy, many searchlights scanned the sky, looking for enemy planes. As blackout was ordered, in every house, people would cover their lampshades with black cloth so no light could be seen from outside.

On clear nights, though, the stars twinkling in the sky were very beautiful.

稲荷のキツネ

　ゆきちゃんの家から五十メートルほど離れた裏山のてっぺんに、三入八幡宮が祭ってあります。
　八幡宮へお参りするには、長い石段を登らなければなりません。表側の石段は二百三十八段もあり、裏側には百九十三段築いてあります。
　八幡宮の山につらなった隣りの小山は丸子山です。丸子山には、古ぼけてうす気味悪い、稲荷神社が祭ってありました。
　八幡宮へ登る、表側の道の中ほどに石の鳥居があり、その鳥居の下に立って手をパン、パンと強く打つと、キャン、キャンと八幡宮が返事をします。
　みんなは、
「気味悪い、稲荷神社に住んでいるキツネが返事をするんじゃあ」と恐ろしがって、夜、八幡宮の表がわの道は小走りで通り抜けていました。

Fox in the *Inari* Shrine

Miiri Hachimangu Shrine was on a hill about 50 meters away from Yuki's house. To get to the shrine, people had to climb a long flight of 238 stone steps. Behind the shrine there was another steep stone stairway with 193 steps.

The small hill next to this Hachimangu Shrine was called Marukoyama. On this hill, there was a grim old *inari** shrine.

There was a path leading to the Hachimangu Shrine, and in the middle of the path there stood a stone *torii*, a shrine gate. When people stood at the *torii* and clapped their hands loudly, they would hear fox-like barking, "Yap, yap, yap" coming from the shrine.

The villagers were frightened and would say, "I'm afraid. The spirit of the fox living in the *inari* shrine is barking back."

At night, they would run when they had to pass in front of the Hachimangu Shrine.

* The god of harvests. People believe the messengers of this god take the form of a fox.

オシッコがしたくなる

　ゆきちゃんの家は小さな山里にあります。

　里の真ん中に川が流れています。

　その川の向う側に、十軒ほどの農家がありました。

　その中の一軒に、鈴木さんの家もあります。

　鈴木のおばさんは、毎晩、夜中の十二時になるとお便所へ行くくせがありました。

　昔の農家の便所は家の外にあったので、夜中に便所へ行くのは少し怖いのです。

　それでも鈴木のおばさんはオシッコを我慢できず、しぶしぶお便所へ行っていました。

　住みなれた家なので、どんな闇夜でも手さぐりでお便所へ行くことができたからです。

The Urge to Pee

Yuki's house was in a small village in the countryside. There was a river running through the village. On the other side of the river there were about ten farmhouses. Mrs. Suzuki's house was one of them.

Mrs. Suzuki was in the habit of going to the toilet around midnight. In those days, farmers used outdoor privies. It was a bit scary to go to the privy late at night, but Mrs. Suzuki couldn't wait, so she had to go.

She knew her house like the back of her hand, so she could feel her way to the privy even on the darkest night.

オレンジ色の火

　今夜も鈴木のおばさんは、十二時になるとオシッコがしたくなりました。

　おばさんは、手さぐりで家の外のお便所へ入って、なにげなく窓から外を見てびっくりしました。

　墨を流したように真っ暗な田んぼでオレンジ色の火が、ゆら〜り、ゆら〜り、ゆれていたからです。

　おばさんはアレ？と思いながらオシッコをすませると、急いで寝床へもぐりこみました。

　次の晩も、お便所へ行って、恐る恐る遠くの田んぼを見ました。

　すると、昨夜と同じ田んぼで、オレンジ色の火が、ゆら〜り、ゆら〜り、ゆれながらうごめいています。

　おばさんの胸はドキドキして、なかなかオシッコができません。

　とうとうオシッコをしないまま、家へ駆込むと頭から布団をかぶって、ふるえながら朝を待ちました。

Orange Flames

One night as usual, Mrs. Suzuki had to go to the privy around midnight. She went out of the house and felt her way to the privy. She happened to look out the window and was shocked by what she saw.

Amid the total darkness of the fields, orange flames were swaying this way and that. She wondered what they could be. She finished peeing and hurried back to bed.

The next night, when she went to the privy, she fearfully looked toward the distant fields. She again saw orange flames swaying and moving about in the same field as the night before.

Her heart was pounding. She was too frightened to pee, so she gave up and ran back into the house. In her bed, she pulled the futon quilt over her head. Trembling with fear, she waited for dawn to come.

ねとぼける

　おばさんは、朝ごはんを食べながら、昨夜見た不思議な火のことを家族に話しました。でもみんなは
「ねとぼけとったんじゃろうー」
と言って相手にしてくれません。鈴木のおばさんはくやしくなって、木の橋を渡り、火の見えた田んぼの辺りを見て回りました。
　でも田んぼには麦や野菜が植えてあるほかは、何一つ変わったところはありません。
　おばさんは首をかしげながら、その晩もドキドキする胸をおさえて、お便所の小さな竹格子の窓から遠くの田んぼを見ました。
　「あっ！おる、おる」
　おばさんは思わず声を出しました。オレンジの火が長い尾を引いて踊っています。火は丸くなって消えたり、ぼぉ～っと尾を引いてついたりして、一か所の田んぼで、うじょうじょ動いています。今までに、こんな不思議な火を見たことはありません。

Half-asleep

At breakfast, she told her family about the strange fire she had seen the night before. Her family didn't take what she said seriously. They said, "You must have been half-asleep."

Mrs. Suzuki was upset and crossed the wooden bridge over the river to look around in the fields where she had seen the fire.

She could see nothing but barley fields and vegetable plots. There was nothing out of the ordinary. She was puzzled.

That night, with a pounding heart, Mrs. Suzuki went to the privy and looked again through the bamboo lattice of the small window to the far field.

"There they are!"

She cried out in spite of herself. The orange flames were dancing, dragging long tails behind them. The flames gathered in the field and moved around. They sometimes became round and then disappeared. Sometimes they appeared dimly, dragging their long tails. She had never seen such strange fires before.

不思議な話し

　次の日、鈴木のおばさんは、隣りの家の奥さんに話しました。
　「毎晩、夜中の十二時になると川向こうの田んぼで不思議な火が踊りを踊るんよぅ、嘘じゃあなぁけえ、見てみんさい」と。
　おばさんは、その晩も綿入れのハンチャ（ハンテン）を着るとお便所の前で火の踊りを見ました。
　その不思議な火はひとつではありません。
　丸まったり、くびれて消えたり、ゆらゆら、うじょうじょしながら、しばらく踊ったあと、一列に並んで静かにあぜ道を八幡宮の方へ向います。
　おばさんは、震える指を折りながら火の数を数えました。
　「ひぃとつ、ふぅたつ、みぃっつ」ゆれる火は五つありました。五つの火は、田んぼから三百メートルほど離れた稲荷の山へ次々と消えて行きました。
　鈴木のおばさんは、稲荷のキツネがあの田んぼで何かの儀式をするんじゃあと思いました。

A Mysterious Story

The next day, Mrs. Suzuki told the woman next door about it.

Mrs. Suzuki said, "Every night, I see strange flames dancing in the field across the river around midnight. It's the truth. Be sure to look."

That night too, standing by the privy and wearing a cotton-padded jacket, Mrs. Suzuki saw the fire dancing.

There was more than one flame. They swarmed together, swaying this way and that, sometimes becoming round and sometimes separating and then disappearing. After a while, they stopped dancing, formed a line and went quietly away along the path across the fields toward the Hachimangu Shrine.

With trembling fingers, Mrs. Suzuki tried to count the flames.

"One, two, three…"

There were five moving flames.

The five flames moved toward the hill about 300 meters away from the field and, one after another. disappeared into the hill where the *inari* shrine was.

Mrs. Suzuki was sure that the fox spirits from the *inari* shrine were performing some kind of ceremony in the field.

逆立った髪の毛

　おばさんは、火が稲荷の山へ消えた後も闇を睨んでいました。
すると暗がりのなかから声がしました。
　「見たよ、見たッ！」と。
　その声に体がギクッと動きます。
　おばさんが闇に目を凝らしてみると、髪の毛を逆立てた隣の奥さんが立っていました。
　それを見たとたん、自分の髪の毛も逆立ってきて、それを見た隣の奥さんもまたびっくりして二人は髪の毛を逆立てたまま、目を見はり歯をガチガチならしました。
　「見た！、見た！、見た！、見た！見た！」
　奥さんは、同じことを言いつづけます。
　女の人が恐ろしい目に会うと髪の毛が逆立つと、祖父から聞いていたが、本当だと鈴木のおばさんは思いました。

Hair Standing on End

Mrs. Suzuki gazed into the dark even after the flames had disappeared into the hill of the *inari* shrine.

Then she heard a voice in the dark.

"I saw them! I saw them!"

The voice made her jump. Mrs. Suzuki peered into the darkness and saw her neighbor standing there, her hair standing on end.

When Mrs. Suzuki saw her, her hair stood on end too. The woman next door was surprised to see it. The two of them stood there, their teeth chattering, their eyes wide open and their hair standing on end.

"I saw them! I saw them! I saw them! I saw them!"

The woman next door kept saying the same thing again and again. Mrs. Suzuki had heard her grandfather say that a shock will make your hair stand on end. How right he was, she thought.

うわさ

　火のうわさは、あっと言う間に川向こうの人たちに広まりました。

　大人は手ぬぐいで頰かむりをすると火鉢に炭火を入れました。

　子どもは防空頭巾をかぶって火鉢の火で手足をあぶりながら、キツネ火の踊りを見るようになりました。

　こうして、何日かが過ぎたある日、

　鈴木のおばさんは、鏡に写る自分の顔がキツネにそっくりだと気づきました。

　「ひょっとして、キツネの魂が自分に乗り移ったんかなぁ」と思いました。

　その証拠に、キツネが山から出てきて踊り終わって山へ帰って行くまで見届けないと寝付かれません。

　自分がキツネになってゆくのを、人にさとられないように気をつけて暮らしました。

Rumors

The rumor of the fires spread rapidly among the villagers on that side of the river.

Adults and children too stayed up to watch the fox fire dance. The adults wrapped their heads and faces with towels and prepared hot charcoal in *hibachi* braziers.

Children wore air-raid hoods and warmed their hands and feet over these stoves. Several nights passed in this way.

One day, as Mrs. Suzuki looked in the mirror she discovered that her face looked like the face of a fox.

"Maybe I am possessed by the spirit of a fox from the *inari* shrine," she thought. Proof of this was the fact that she became restless at night and could not sleep until she saw the foxes come out of the hill, finish dancing and go back to the hill.

She tried not to let anyone know that she was turning into a fox.

小一郎
  さて、話しは変わって。

  ゆきちゃんのお父さんの名前は、小一郎です。

  小一郎は、年寄りだったので、戦争に行きませんでした。

  そのかわり、お国のために一生懸命、仕事をします。

  ある日、小一郎は仕事から帰るなり

  「わっ、はっ、は、は、はぁー」と、笑いころげました。

  「川の向こうじゃぁ、毎晩、火鉢の火で手足しゅう、あぶってのう、キツネの火踊りゅう見よるんじゃげなでぇ、そのキツネャぁ、なんと、うちの田んぼで踊りゅう踊るんじゃげなぁー、わっ、はっ、は、は、はぁー」

  と、大笑いします。

  ゆきちゃんは、うちの田んぼが、これほどの噂になっていようとは夢にも思いませんでした。

Koichiro

Not to change the subject…

Koichiro was Yuki's father. He was too old to be drafted, but he worked hard for his country.

One day, when Koichiro came home from work, he burst into laughter.

"Ha, ha, ha, ha!" He laughed hard and said, "On the other side of the river, I hear that every night people are taking out their braziers to warm their hands and feet to watch some fox fire dance. Believe it or not, they are saying that the foxes dance in our field. Ha, ha, ha!"

Yuki had no idea that her family's field was the talk of the village.

ふえたキツネ

　ゆきちゃんが、うちの田んぼで、キツネが火の踊りを踊ると知った夜のことです。
　川向こうの人たちは、今夜も、キツネの親子が稲荷の山から出てくるのを今か今かと待っていました。
　すると暗い山から、一列に並んだ十匹のキツネ火が怪しげに動きながら出てきました。

　「大変だ、大変だ。五匹だったキツネ火が、たった一晩で十匹に増えた。おまけに、子どものキツネ火が遠くまで飛び跳ていく。こりゃぁ〜、大事が起きる証拠じゃあー」
　と、顔色を変えておびえます。
　十匹のキツネ火は、狂ったように踊りまくります。
　その狂ったような踊りを見ていると、鈴木のおばさんの顔はますます、とがってゆきました。

More Foxes

It was the night after Yuki had heard that there were fox fire dances in her family's field.

The villagers on the other side of the village were again eagerly waiting for the fox family to come out of the hill of the *inari* shrine.

They saw ten fox fires come out from the dark hill, moving mysteriously in a line.

"Goodness gracious! Until yesterday there were five, but now there are ten foxes! What's more, the little ones are running so far afield. This must be an omen of something terrible that's about to happen." They were pale with fear.

The ten fox fires were dancing in a frenzy.

As she watched the frantic dance, Mrs. Suzuki's face became more pointed than ever.

いも団子

　キツネが十匹に増えた次の朝、鈴木のおばさんは、急いで芋団子を作りました。

　そして、うす気味悪い稲荷神社へお参りすると、恐る恐る荒れたやしろの掃除をして、作ったばかりの芋団子をそなえながら

　「どうか、お静まりください」と、祈りました。

　でもキツネは、ますます怪しげに踊りを踊ります。川向こうの人たちも、知らず知らず頭をふってキツネ火の真似をしました。

Potato Dumplings

　The morning after the foxes increased to ten, Mrs. Suzuki hurriedly made potato dumplings and went to the dreaded *inari* shrine. After timidly cleaning the spooky shrine, she offered the freshly made potato dumplings to the shrine and prayed, "Please calm down, please."

　Despite this, the foxes danced even more ominously.

　Without realizing it, the villagers on the other side of the river were shaking their heads from side to side, just like the fox fires.

ヨトウ虫

　ゆきちゃんの家では、稲を刈った後の田んぼに、麦とぶんどう豆（グリンピースの一種）の種をまきました。

　ぶんどう豆は、田んぼの約七十坪に植えました。

　麦もぶんどう豆も、芽を出して寒い冬をこしました。

　川土手の、猫柳がビロードの花芽を出し、やがて桃の花が咲きそろうと、土の中に隠れていたヨトウ虫（夜盗虫）が目を覚まします。

　ヨトウ虫はヨトウ蛾の幼虫です。幼虫は体長、四センチほどある、茶色い虫です。

　夜になると、土の中からはい出てきて豆の葉を食い荒らします。

Cutworms

Yuki's family had planted barley and green peas in their field after they harvested rice. The green peas were planted in one corner of the rice field.

Both the barley and the green peas survived the cold winter, and now they were sprouting.

The pussy willows on the riverbank were burgeoning with velvet buds, and the peach trees came into full bloom. This was the season when cutworms came out of the earth where they had hidden.

Cutworms are the caterpillars of cabbage moths. They are brown and about four centimeters long. They crawl out of the earth at night and eat the leaves of pea plants.

ゆきちゃんの家族は五人です。

　お父さんの小一郎は、毎晩、夜中の十一時半になると五本のタイマツに火をつけました。

　ゆきちゃんたちは、火のついたタイマツを一人が一本ずつ持って、田んぼへ行くと、タイマツの明かりで、ぶんどう豆の茎を照らしてヨトウ虫をさがしました。

　豆の茎にたかっているヨトウ虫を見つけると、竹の箸で摘んで取り、腰に下げている空き缶に入れました。

　こうして、ゆきちゃんの家族は、夜な夜なヨトウ虫退治をしていたのです。

　この時代は、どんな虫も手で取らなければなりませんでした。

There were five people in Yuki's family.

Every night, at eleven thirty, Yuki's father, Koichiro, lit five torches. Each of the family members carried a torch and went to their field.

They cast the torchlight over the pea stems and looked for cutworms. When they found cutworms on the pea stems, they picked them off with bamboo chopsticks and put them in the empty cans tied to their waists.

Every night, in this way, Yuki's family tried to get rid of cutworms.

In those days, people had to get rid of harmful bugs by hand.

いたずら

　いたずら好きの小一郎は、川向こうの人たちがキツネの火踊りに夢中だと知った夜から、五本だったタイマツを十本に増やして火をつけました。

　灯火管制がしかれているというのに「こんな山里なんかに敵は来ん」と言いながら火のついたタイマツを二本ずつゆきちゃんたちにわたしてくれました。

　三匹の子ギツネは、防空頭巾をかぶって綿入れのハンチャを着ると、わらぞうりを履き、しもやけで風船のようにはれた小さな手に、火のついたタイマツを二本ずつ持って、

「小一郎ぎつねの、お出ましぃ、お出でましぃ〜」

と歌いながら、田んぼへ行って、虫を取りました。

「川向こうの人たちは、この火をキツネの火だと思いこんで、夢中で見ているだろう」と思うと、面白くてたまりません。

　ゆきちゃんと二人の妹は、毎晩寝床から飛び起きて、タイマツの火を怪しげに振り回して楽しく虫を取り、川向こうの人たちをだまし続けました。

Tricks

Koichiro loved playing tricks on people. The night after he learned that the villagers on the other side of the river were excited about the fox fire dance, he increased the number of torches from five to ten.

Blackout had been ordered, but he said, "The enemy would not come so deep into the counyryside," and handed the torches to Yuki and her sisters, two for each.

The three little foxes were wearing cotton-padded jackets, air-raid hoods and straw sandals, each carrying two torches in their little hands, which were swollen like balloons with chilblains.

They sang, "Fox Koichiro is here! Fox Koichiro is here!" and went to the field to pick off cutworms. It was great fun for them to imagine how excited the villagers on the other side of the river must be, watching the flames of the torches and believing they were fox fires.

Every night, Yuki and her two little sisters jumped out of bed. They had fun picking off the cutworms and spookily swinging their torches. They kept playing this trick on the villagers.

消えたキツネ火

　そんなこととはつゆ知らず、川向こうの人たちは、キツネの火踊りに夢中です。

　ゆきちゃんの家族も、夢中で火の踊りを踊って、虫を取りました。

　おかげで、ヨトウ虫はいなくなりました。

　そして親子ギツネも出なくなりました。

　親子ギツネが出なくなって、川向こうの人たちは心配しました。

　稲荷のキツネに何かが起きたのかなぁと。

　自分たちも夜中の楽しみが無くなって淋しくてたまりません。みんなは家の柱に掛けてある振り子時計が夜の十二時を打つと、外を見るくせがついていました。

No More Fox Fires

The villagers on the other side of the river were beside themselves with excitement as they watched the fox fire dance, without knowing the truth of it.

Yuki and her family were also excited, dancing the fox fire dance and looking for cutworms.

Soon the cutworms had all been got rid of, and the fox parents and cubs also disappeared.

After the foxes disappeared, the villagers across the river were worried about what had happened to the foxes of the *inari* shrine. Now that the midnight excitement had ended, people felt downhearted.

They were still in the habit of looking outside at midnight when the pendulum clocks hanging on the walls of their houses struck twelve.

化けの皮

　小一郎ぎつねが出なくなって何日かが過ぎたある日、
　鈴木のおばさんはゆきちゃんの家に来て、小一郎に言いました。
　「あんたん家の田んぼで、毎晩、稲荷のキツネが火の踊りゅう踊りよりましたで」と。
　すると小一郎は
　「そのキツネ火やぁ、わしの一家がヨトウ虫を取りよった火でがんす」と言うと、鈴木のおばさんは、ぶったまげて、その場へふにゃふにゃぁと、座り込みました。
　ゆきちゃんは、悪い事をしたと思いました。
　でも、お父さんの小一郎は、
　「キツネ火の正体見たり、タイマツの火」と歌って
　「わっはっはっはぁー」と笑い転げます。
　とうとう火の正体が、ゆきちゃんたちの仕業だったと、化けの皮ははがれてしまいました。
　川向こうの人たちは、あきれるやら安心するやらで、にが笑いしました。
　やがて鈴木のおばさんからキツネの魂がぬけてゆき、もとの優しい顔にもどりました。

Truth Revealed

A few days after Fox Koichiro stopped appearing, Mrs. Suzuki came to Yuki's house and said to Koichiro, "Night after night, we saw the foxes of the *inari* shrine dancing in your field."

Koichiro said, "The fox fires must have been the torches we were carrying when we were working in the field to get rid of cutworms."

Hearing this, Mrs. Suzuki sank to the ground in shock.

Yuki felt sorry for what they had done, but Koichiro joked about it, singing, "The foxes are out of the bag, they were only a torch flame rag!" and laughed his hearty laugh.

Now the the people knew the truth. The fox fires were actually made by Yuki's family.

The villagers across the river were dumbfounded, but they were relieved and smiled embarrassed smiles.

Soon the fox spirit left Mrs. Suzuki, and her face returned to the normal face of a kind woman again.

ほんのり、しあわせ

　寒い冬の眠りからさめた桜が花を咲かせアッという間に散ると、野山がほんのり黄緑に染まりました。

　やがて、つややかな緑薫る五月がくると、ぶんどう豆が大きな実をつけました。

　豆の実をさやから出して煮て食べると、ぼわんと甘い味が口の中に広がって、ほんのりしあわせな気持ちになります。

　ぶんどう豆は、麦ばっかりのご飯に入れて炊いて食

Small Happiness

　The cherry trees awoke from their cold winter sleep and bloomed. In no time, the blossoms were gone, and the hills and fields were tinged with light green.

　In May, when the hills and villages were richly fresh and green, Yuki's family harvested the big green peas.

　When they took the peas from the pods and cooked them, the peas tasted faintly sweet. The sweet taste made them feel happy. They cooked the green peas with barley and ate them.

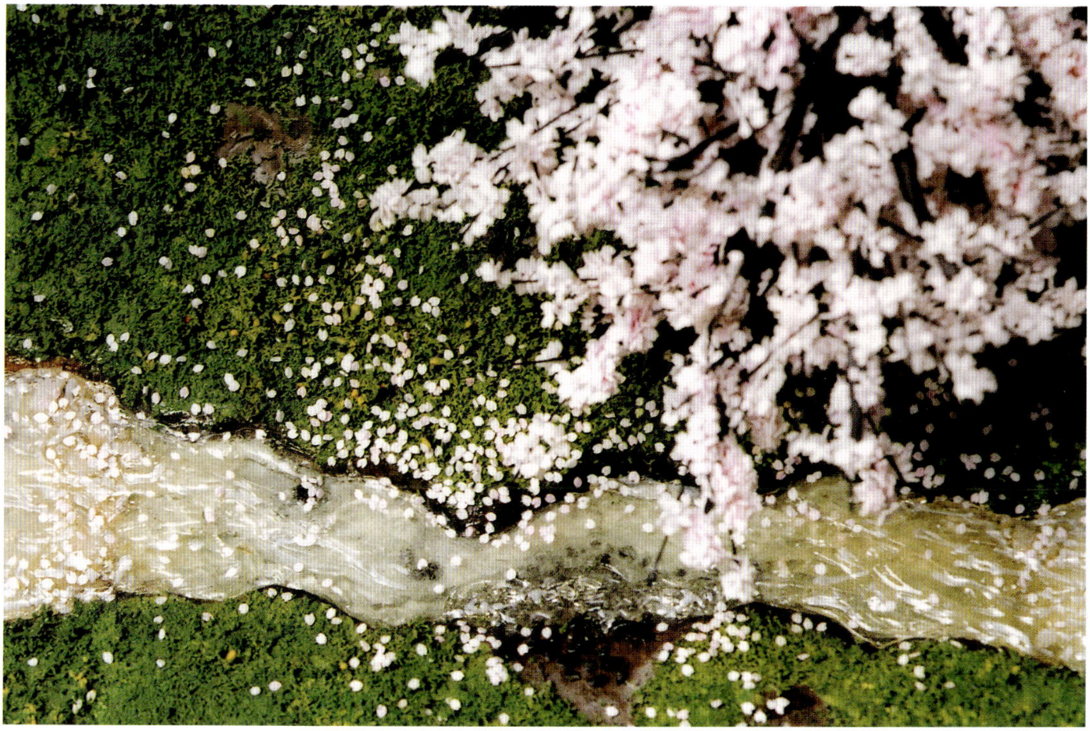

べました。

　そして豆をとった後の田んぼに、水を張って稲の苗を植えました。

　田や畑で蛙が「グワ、グワ」鳴いて、スマートなツバメはそこらじゅうを飛びかいます。

　足先の丸いカジカは、川原で鈴をころがすように「コロコロコロ」と鳴き、日が沈むとメダカが泳ぐ川辺で、たくさんの蛍が光を放ちます。

　でも夜空は何本ものサーチライトがぐるぐる回って、敵の飛行機を監視していました。

　村役場のサイレンは空襲警報を鳴らしては、解除のサイレンを鳴らして、戦争の危険が迫っていると知らせていました。

　昼も夜も敵の大型爆撃機B29が、広島の空に飛んで来るようになりました。

　でもB29は広島へ爆弾を落としませんでした。
　ゆきちゃんたちは油断していました。

After the green peas were harvested, they flooded the fields with water and planted rice seedlings.

Frogs croaked in the rice paddies and vegetable fields, and swallows swooped gracefully all around.

Kajika frogs with round toes sang on the riverbed in their tinkling voices.

After dark, hundreds of fireflies glowed on and off along the river where the killifish swam.

But still night after night searchlights scanned the night sky looking for enemy planes.

The siren at the village hall sounded air-raid warnings and all clear signals, reminding people of the ever-present dangers of war.

Day and night, throughout the war, large B-29 enemy planes frequently flew over Hiroshima. They didn't drop bombs on Hiroshima, though.

Yuki and her family thought they would be all right.

ピカドン

1945年8月6日午前8時15分
晴(は)れ渡(わた)った夏の朝でした。
山里は蟬(せみ)がやかましく鳴いていました。
突然(とつぜん)、空に小さな雲がひとつ湧(わ)き出てきました。
それは、三つに分かれて、大きくなりながら降(お)りてくる不思議な雲でした。

Pikadon

Eight fifteen, on the morning of August 6th, 1945...
It was a fine summer morning.
Cicadas were singing loudly in the village.
In the clear blue sky, Yuki spotted a little cloud. The strange cloud turned into three little clouds that got bigger and bigger as they came down.

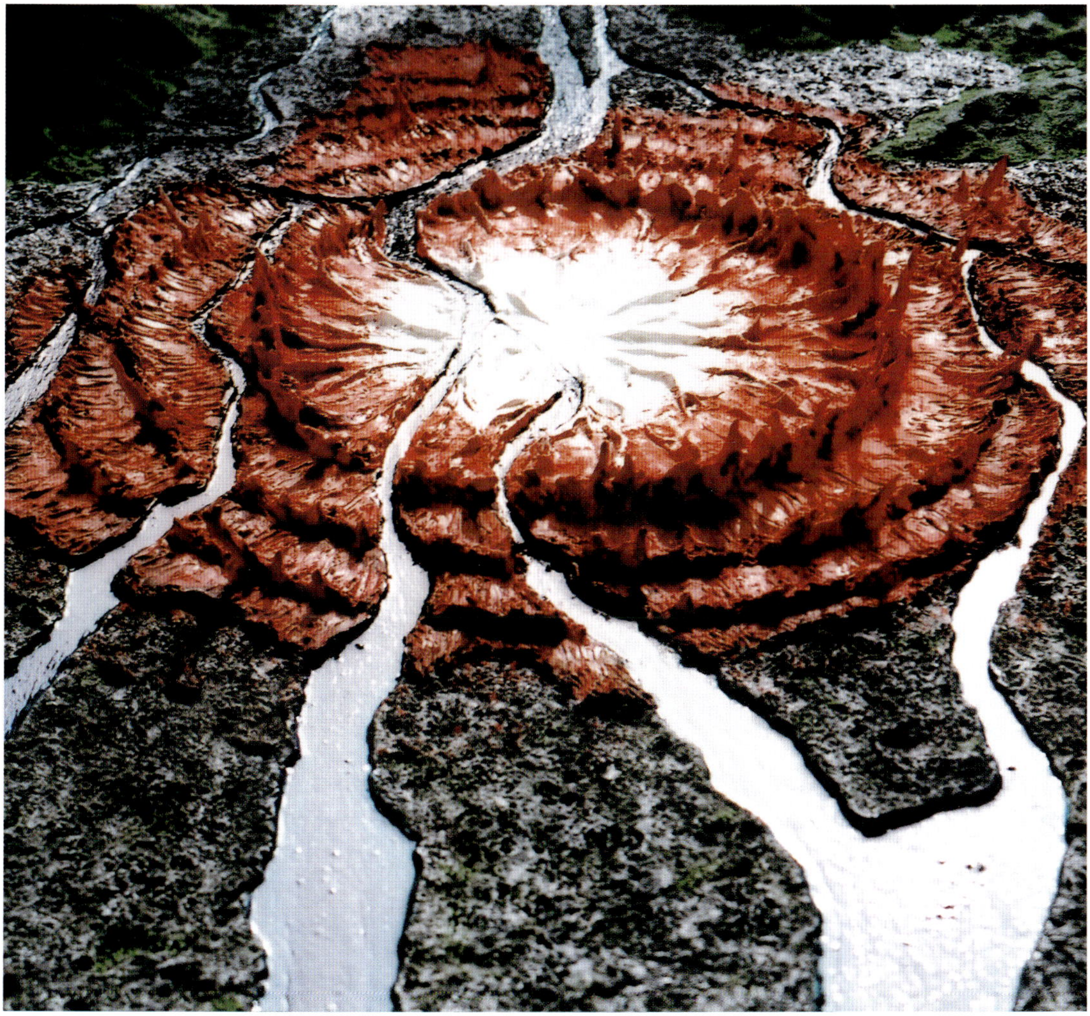

その不思議な雲を見ていると、空がパッと光ってドンと音がして風が一筋、波のように吹いてきました。

　ゆきちゃんが音のしたほうを見ると、山と山の間にものすごい入道雲がもくもく湧き出てきました。

　すると、太陽が薄黄色の線を引いて村じゅうに射しました。頭の上を見ると、三つの雲は三つの落下傘に変わってゆっくりゆっくり隣村の亀山へ落ちていきました。強い光は広島の人も、建物も、動物も、木の根っこまでも焼きつくして街は瓦礫となりました。

　ゆきちゃんたちは、光爆弾のことをピカドンと名をつけました。

　ピカドンで生き残った人の苦しみはいつまでも続きます。

　ゆきちゃんたちが見た、三つの落下傘は、ピカドンの自動観測装置だったのです。

Then she saw a tremendous flash of light and heard a roaring sound.

Yuki felt a gust of wind sweep over her like a wave.

When she turned toward the direction of the sound, she saw a gigantic cloud towering over the mountains.

Then the entire village was covered with light yellow sunbeams.

She looked up and saw the three little clouds turn into three parachutes and slowly land in Kameyama near Yuki's village.

People, buildings, animals, birds — even the roots of trees — were burned up by the intense light. Hiroshima was reduced to rubble.

People called the flash bomb "Pikadon."

The sufferings of the survivors would never end.

The three parachutes Yuki saw were carrying observation equipment for the Pikadon.

丸子山の稲荷神社

　戦争が終わって平和になり数えきれない年月がたちました。

　鈴木のおばさんもお父さんの小一郎も、とっくの昔に天国の人になりました。

　村だった、ゆきちゃんのすんでいる山里も広島市になって、道という道に街灯がつけられ、月の出ない闇夜も明るくなって、夜道も安心して歩けます。

　稲荷神社が祭ってある丸子山は、相変わらず怪しい雰囲気がしていました。

　丸子山にブルドーザーが入り、宅地の開発がはじまりました。

　山が削られて平になっていくうち、いくつもの遺跡（墳墓）が発掘されました。二千年の眠りから覚めた墳墓の中に、珍しいいも貝の腕輪をはめた女性の墳墓もあり、ひろしまの卑弥呼と言われています。

　その女性の墳墓に寄り添うように子どもの墳墓もあり、ゆきちゃんたちをドキドキさせました。

Inari Shrine on Marukoyama Hill

The war ended, and peaceful days returned. Many years have passed since then.

Mrs. Suzuki and Yuki's father Koichiro went to heaven long ago.

Yuki's neighborhood was a small village then, but now it is part of Hiroshima City. There are street lamps on every street. The streets are well lit, so people are no longer afraid to walk outside, even on moonless nights.

Marukoyama Hill, on which the *inari* shrine stood, still had a grim atmosphere.

Bulldozers were brought in to build a housing development, and when the hill was leveled off many ancient graves were uncovered after a sleep of 2000 years.

In one of these graves, they found the remains of a woman wearing a bracelet made of rare Conus shells. She was called the Himiko* of Hiroshima.

A child's grave was also found next to her grave. Yuki and the townspeople were excited about this discovery.

*A queen of Japan in ancient times

永遠の鳴き声

　遺跡が出た丸子山にはたくさんの住宅が建ちました。

　あやしげな稲荷神社は住宅の横へ移されて、ひそかにゆきちゃんたちを見守っています。

　三入八幡宮は、相変わらず長い石段の上に祭ってあります。

　八幡宮の釣鐘（梵鐘）は、世界大戦のとき国に供出されて鉄砲の弾になるはずでしたが、宝物だったので誰かが隠していました。

　戦争が終わったので、八幡宮へ戻されました。

　今も三入八幡宮へ登る鳥居の下で手をパン、パンと強く打つと、キャン、キャンと怪しく返事をしてくれます。

　三入八幡宮はこれからも、手をたたくと釣鐘の音とともに、キャン、キャンと鳴き続けることでしょう。

　ゆきちゃんは、もういっぺん「小一郎ぎつね」になりたいなぁと思います。

　これで、ゆきちゃんのお話は終わります。

Eternal Voice

Many houses were built on Marukoyama Hill, where the ruins were excavated.

The grim *inari* shrine was relocated next to the newly built houses where it silently watches over the people.

Miiri Hachimangu Shrine is still at the top of a long flight of stone steps.

The hanging bell of the Hachimangu Shrine had been ordered to be given to the government during the Second World War to be melted down into bullets, but because it was a precious treasure, somebody had hidden the bell. After the war, the bell was returned to the Hachimangu Shrine.

Even today, when people clap their hands loudly under the *torii* gate at the bottom of the steps of the Hachimangu Shrine, they hear the shrine ominously bark back, "Yap, yap, yap!"

Miiri Hachimangu Shrine will forever bark back at people who clap their hands, and the sound of the bell will continue to be heard.

Yuki thinks it would be nice if she could play Fox Koichiro again.

This is the end of Yuki's story.

あとがき

　「小一郎ぎつね」は、私の体験を本にしたものです。
　第二次世界大戦の終わりごろでした。
　灯火管制がしかれて、家の明かりは一点も外へ漏らさないようにして暮らしていました。
　甘いものはなく、甘味のある野菜を作って食べるのがささやかな贅沢でした。
　干し柿・さつまいも・たまねぎ・豆類。
　戦争のために殺虫剤がなくて、あらゆる虫は手で取っていました。
　夜盗虫は夜中に活動します。
　早いものは四月に孵化して夜盗蛾になります。
　夜中の害虫駆除は、母もわたしも二人の妹にもつらい仕事でした。
　幸いにも、川向こうの人たちがキツネ火の踊りを楽しんでいると知ったので、仕事が楽しくなりました。
　戦争中はこれと言った娯楽の無い時代です。
　まさか小一郎ぎつねが川向こうの人たちを楽しませているなど、夢にも思いませんでした。

　でもあの時代の自然は美しく、のどかでした。
　山は青く川は清く空気はおいしく
　小一郎ぎつねは、こんな時代の話です。
　丸子山の墳墓と貝の腕輪は実物を見ることができます。
　三入八幡宮は今も、梵鐘の音とともに、キャン、キャンと鳴いてくれます。
　これからも、永遠に鳴き続けることでしょう。

Afterword

"Fox Koichiro" is based on on my own experiences.

It took place near the end of the Second World War.

Blackout was in force. At night, people tried to prevent any light from being seen from their houses.

There were no sweets then. A simple pleasure was to grow sweet vegetables to eat.

Dried persimmons, sweet potatoes, onions and beans.

During the war, there was no pesticide, and people had to remove various bugs all by hand. Cutworms come out at night. The early ones emerge in April and become cabbage moths.

My mother, my two sisters and I found it hard work to pick off cutworms in the middle of the night.

Fortunately as we came to know that the villagers on the other side of the river had become excited about the fox fire dance, we had fun doing the work.

People did not have much entertainment during the war. We had no idea that Fox Koichiro would entertain the people across the river.

In those days, the nature around us was beautiful and gentle. The hills were green, the river was clean, and the air was delicious.

"Fox Koichiro" is a story of those days.

You can see the actual graves of Marukoyama Hill and the shell bracelet.

Miiri Hachimangu Shrine still replies to people, barking "Yap, yap, yap!" and you can hear the bell. The sounds of the shrine will be heard forever.

作者	森本マリア
翻訳	小泉直子
翻訳チェック	ジム・ロナルド　ナンシー・H・ロス
立体挿絵	彩瀬ひよ子

"Fox Koichiro"
Written by Maria Morimoto
Translated into English by Naoko Koizumi
With assistance from Jim Ronald and Nancy H. Ross
Figures were created by Hiyoko Ayase

小一郎ぎつね
<small>こいちろう</small>

2006年11月22日　発行

著者　　森本マリア
発行　　吉備人出版
　　　　〒700-0823　岡山市丸の内2丁目11-22
　　　　電話086-235-3456　ファクス086-234-3210
　　　　http://www.kibito.co.jp
　　　　mail:books@kibito.co.jp

印刷所　　広和印刷株式会社
製本所　　日宝綜合製本株式会社

乱丁本・落丁本はお取り替えいたします。ご面倒ですが小社までご返送ください。
定価はカバーに表示しています。
ⒸMorimoto Maria 2006, Printed in Japan
ISBN4-86069-148-2　C0093